K.M. ROBINSON

AND THEY'LL COME HOME

The Legends Chronicles

LITTLE BO PEEP

Little Bo Peep has lost her sheep
and doesn't know where to find them.
Leave them alone
and they'll come home,
wagging their tails behind them.

CHAPTER 1

"YOU SHOULDN'T HAVE DONE THAT." The man grinned at Peep, eyes narrowing when she glared back. "That was a bad choice."

"So was your outfit," Peep hissed. Her fingers curled like cat claws behind her back, only stretching as far as the zip ties would allow. The plastic bit into her skin.

"Settle down, young one. You're going to be here for a while, so you might as well get comfortable," he smirked at her. "Or at least as comfortable as you *can.*"

The bag over Peep's head had knocked her hair in her face, pieces of it still lingered, dancing in front of her because of the static caused by the bag being ripped away. She blew a quick puff of air, hoping to move the annoying strands.

"What do you want, Piper?" Peep growled.

"Oh," Piper drawled, "so you know me. Your boss taught you well, I see."

Boss?

"Shame," he continued. "I would have loved to have offered you a job. You'd have been happy on my team, Peep. Ah, well…we work with what we have.

"Settle in, Peep," he walked around her, inspecting her. "Oh. Should I call you *Bo*?"

If her uncle were still alive, she would have decked him for talking her mother into that name. She hated it *and* the girlfriend that inspired her uncle just long enough to name her before she disappeared a few days later. That woman never should have been let near the pregnant lady.

Piper turned and walked out the door, leaving Peep to sit in silence. The moment he was gone, Peep pulled at her wrists, trying to free herself. Her arm brushed against a chair as a scraping noise filled the large room.

When she couldn't break it, she turned her attention to finding an escape once she found the upper hand. The room was brighter than it should have been as the light shifted in through the minimalist windows high above. Metal walls grew into an unimpressive point in the center of the ceiling. The room had a slight blue tint to it. Though nothing like the glow of computer screens, that too was there.

Peep shivered as a cool breeze blew across the floor from where Piper had opened the door moments ago. The hall must be freezing if it were still so strong. The shivering didn't help break the restraint, even though it might have been violent enough.

As quietly as she could, Peep scooted across the floor, making sure there were no motion sensors or cameras watching her. She assumed if there had been, her movements would have caused someone to check on her; that or they wanted to see how she would try to escape.

Instead, she made her way to a cushier office chair. Laying her head down on the seat, she rested on the floor, waiting for Piper to return. The puffy cap sleeve poked her annoyingly in the face. Her eyes memorized every inch of the room, calculating an escape, searching for weapons, and hoping she could survive her captivity.

She noted a few places to be careful. Knowing Piper, she assumed torture wasn't out of the question. She pinpointed exactly where she needed to never set foot.

Peep curled her legs up around her, sitting sideways so she didn't throw her back out—*the last thing she needed* —and took a deep breath. Her uncle always told her to breathe deeply when she needed to focus and stay alert.

"The mind gets foggy," she whispered, not bothering to finish the thought. No need to give Piper the idea of restricting her airflow and helping the foggy process along.

Minutes passed. Peep's mind wanted to drift, but she held her focus. She wouldn't give Piper the upper hand.

Finally, the door opened again. Piper closed it behind

him as he strode toward Peep. He brushed by a table, knocking into a pad of paper on a clipboard sitting on the edge. A metal marble bounced to the ground, rolling across the hard floor. It scraped along, irritating Peep.

"When I said to make yourself comfortable, I didn't actually think you'd do it," Piper commented, picking up the clipboard. "Now, Peep, we need to have a little conversation.

"I need to know about the Legends—"

"No."

"Tsk, tsk, Peep. I wasn't finished," he chastised her. "I need to know how to reach them."

"I don't know." She leveled a glare at him as he pulled up a chair and sat in front of her.

Peep straightened when he shifted closer, propping her elbow up on the chair behind her. It rolled half an inch back. She gripped her wrists to steady herself, wrapping her fingers around them as one wrist rested on top of the other. Piper eyed her.

"I want to talk to Muffet," he tried again.

"And I want to talk to the man who developed the Irex system, but we can't always get what we want, now can we?"

"Listen up, Peep. You don't have to make this hard on yourself. You can move on from this rather quickly. All you have to do is tell me how to reach Muffet."

"No." Peep lifted her top leg and kicked out,

connecting with Piper's shin.

They yelped at the same time; Piper in pain, Peep in surprise as the chair kicked out from behind her. She righted herself before Piper could, swinging back to watch him falter.

The door burst open, slamming against the metallic walls as she righted herself. The man that entered was tall and built. Peep only had enough time to take stock of his large arms and black muscle shirt before Piper ordered him out.

Piper turned his attention to Peep.

"You failed, Peep," he commented, crossing his arm over his knee, still rubbing the spot where she had kicked him. "The good news is that I don't need you. I already know how to reach your boss. I just needed to find out if you were going to play along or not. I guess we'll have to do this the more complicated way."

He sighed as if he actually cared what her decision had been.

"No matter. Let me tell you how this is going to go." Piper gave her a terse smile.

"We're about to send Muffet on a little mission. You see, I have certain things that need to be accomplished rather quickly. Now I *could* do them myself, but it's so much easier to let her do all the work. I'm convinced she has access to some things I can't get a hold of at the moment anyway.

"In a few minutes, we're going to call her, you and I. We're going to make sure she is properly motivated.

"I need Muffet to do my dirty work, Peep, but I also need *her*."

"Why?" Peep cut him off as he paused for a breath.

"She's the leader of the Legends, Peep. She has something I need."

Peeps mind swirled, the entire room bobbing in a grand sweeping motion. What did he want?

"I can see you're trying to work this out, *little girl,* but you're wasting your time. Only the leader of the Legends knows."

Suddenly, she knew exactly what he wanted. She also realized that Fet's plan to act like the leader of the Legends had worked. They had tricked even Piper. Fet had been brilliant to suggest taking the lead and acting as Peep's shield in preparation for something like this to ever happen.

How easy it would have been for Piper to win. He had Peep. She had no escape… and she had all the answers.

Distraction would be her friend now.

"Time to earn your keep, little girl."

Piper reached down and grabbed Peep's elbow, jerking her to her feet. She unsteadily got her feet beneath her just before Piper dragged his chair over and slammed her into it.

"Here we go," Piper sang as he clicked the device into

a tripod to steady it.

Peep glared at him as he lifted his device and made contact.

"Behave," he warned. "Tell her to cooperate, or you will be hurt. Tell her you fear for your life. Do whatever you need to do, just move her into action. I wanted this handled today."

A beep sounded, followed by static as someone outside let Piper know they had turned their cloaking device on. It sizzled through the air. Whatever Piper said would be digitally altered. She assumed it had been set specifically to his voice and wouldn't change hers since Fet actually needed to hear her.

Piper watched the screen, looking up at her only when it came alive with light, indicating that they were live. The noise of the Legends' headquarters filled the room. She could hear T and BB talking in the background. Her boyfriend sounded annoyed.

"Muffet, don't do it!" Peep screeched. She didn't know how to warn Fet that Piper was behind her kidnapping, but she hoped Fet would notice she had purposely used the longer version of her name. That, at least, should have indicated that more was at play.

Piper sneered at her, lunging forward to slap her. His hand stung as it connected with her skin. Peep fell out of the chair, slamming into the ground, taking the brunt of it on her shoulder. She would hurt later.

As she attempted to right herself, she thought she registered a gasp in the background, but couldn't tell who it was.

"Hello again, Muffet. I see you received my first message. So glad we could connect. If you want your lackey alive, crack the code, fix the problem. I'll be in touch with your first puzzle," Piper said gleefully. He was overwhelmingly delighted at the idea of sending Fet on a wild goose chase to save Peep. She knew Piper would never actually let her go.

"Muffet, don't. Get out! *Now!*" Peep screamed, praying she wouldn't get cut off.

Piper backhanded her, this time sending Peep crashing into the chair she had just vacated.

"You stupid girl," Piper bellowed, stalking over to his device to make sure the recording was off.

When he discovered that his lackey had controlled the demise of the feed, he looked up, glaring at Peep. Heavy footsteps pounded toward her and she braced herself, eyes clamping shut despite her wishes.

Piper grabbed Peep's purple-tipped hair, dragging her up. She fought to find her footing as her hair was nearly ripped from her skull.

"You'll pay for that," he spat at her.

"I'm sure I will," Peep taunted through gritted teeth.

His breath was hot against her face. She cringed as he

lingered, allowing his rage to calm down before addressing her again.

Piper dropped her hair and used his hand to slam down on her shoulder, forcing her back into the chair. She didn't fight.

He straightened his shoulders, taking a deep breath. Without another word, he spun on his heels and stomped out of the room, leaving Peep to attempt to control her shaking.

Once he was gone, her eyes darted around the room. Piper had taken his device with him and all other technology seemed to be on lockdown. She wouldn't have been able to hack it with her hands behind her back anyway.

The slow creak of the door drew her attention. A man walked in, slowly approaching her. It was the same muscle-head from before.

He stepped toward her cautiously, as if she might bite him at any moment. He was at least three times her size and towered a foot above her. Red hair stuck out from his arms, goose bumps running the length of his skin from the chill in the room. His short-trimmed beard twitched when he set his jaw.

"Easy," he warned her, only two steps away.

Panic coursed through her. *This wasn't right.*

The thought slipped away as the rag covered her face, lulling her into darkness.

CHAPTER 2

"YOU'RE OKAY," A VOICE COAXED her awake. "Open your eyes."

White light filtered softly into the room beyond the bars. In a world filled with sliding doors and automation, the metal restraints were practically archaic.

Peep held still, allowing her eyes to search the space as the voice continued.

"There you go," he said. "That's it, pick your head up. You've got this."

There was no point in pretending not to hear. She sat up, twisting in place.

"And you are?" she asked in a voice her boyfriend would have rolled his eyes at. He didn't like it when she mimicked Fet's deadpan annoyance.

He waved her over to the bars, beckoning her to join him. With a dramatic sigh, she crawled over close enough to be just out of reach should he try to put his hands through the bars. As she moved, she searched him for weapons. Peep wouldn't put it past anyone to be hiding a syringe or an implant gun in this place. The last thing she needed was to be chipped.

Peep quickly pulled back, realizing she could have been chipped at any point while unconscious. In a panic, she checked her wrists, felt along her neck, and attempted to check her back.

Her tongue ran over her teeth, looking for anything planted there. Nothing felt out of place. Her heart slammed into her ribs as she realized the man was watching her.

"I'm not here to put on a show, you jerk," she yelped at him, realizing she was contorting her body to try to check for a chip.

"They didn't chip you," he replied, "assuming that's what you're looking for. They didn't chip me either."

"That you know of," Peep snarled.

"*I've* never been unconscious," he contradicted her.

Peep looked him up and down as he sat on the ground by the bars that separated them. He had large arms and wore a black shirt. Black was the color of the day, it seemed. His dark hair was cropped close to his head. It made his eyes sparkle.

He looked sadly at her.

"As far as I can tell, you're okay. They dropped you in here two or so hours ago."

"Who are you?" Peep punctuated her words, unwilling to let this little game go on any longer.

"My name is Arach. Who are you?"

Peep raised an eyebrow at him.

He tipped his head giving her an incredulous look.

"Really?" he asked.

Peep snorted. She wasn't about to tell this stranger who she was. For all she knew, Piper had planted him there.

"Fine," Arach shrugged. "Why are you here?"

Peep continued to stare.

"You have to answer me sometime," Arach commented. "If Piper has you down here, it means you're in trouble. We need to stick together."

"If you're so knowledgeable about Piper and his little lair, then why are you still here? Why haven't you found a way out?"

"I have my reasons."

"Now who's being secretive?" Peep said, her words laced with venom.

"My brother works for Piper," Arach admitted. "He worked very hard to make sure I was taken care of when Piper caught me. If I act out, it might come back on him. I may not agree with Piper, but I won't let my brother get hurt because of me."

"So your big plan is just to sit around here all day?" Peep questioned.

"Maybe." Arach lifted a leg up, propping his elbow on his knee as he wrapped his other leg around his ankle. He leaned forward just slightly, trying to engage Peep. "What's your plan?"

"I just woke up. No plan yet."

"Not having a plan could get you killed around here."

"So I figured," Peep tipped her head, trying to figure the man out.

"See this?" Arach asked, holding something out to her. "My brother designed this. It masks us. As long as Piper's men aren't in the room, they have no idea what is going on. It alters their audio and video feeds. For all they know, we're ignoring each other nicely."

It had to be a trap.

"I'm not trying to trick you. I think I know who you are," Arach scooted closer. "I think you work for the Legends... I think you're Pip."

She internally rolled her eyes at his mistake.

"We have a mutual friend," Arach started.

"Oh?" Peep acted uninterested.

A noise sounded in the distance. Footsteps drew closer as Arach's expression changed from laid back to worried.

"Back," Arach waved. "Over there. Act like you're still out."

Arach threw himself backward, tapping the device he had shown Peep, possibly re-engaging the camera system for when they were joined by Piper's men. His frantic movements prompted Peep into action. She flung herself back across her cell, hair flinging over her arm as she hit the floor.

"Bo, you have to be careful with that hair," her uncle used to say when she was little. "One day you're going to get tangled up in it and never be able to get out."

Peep had cut it the next day. The longer pieces still fell in her face when not styled properly.

She slammed her eyes shut, listening intently as the men walked to their cells. They paused outside her door, kicking the bars.

"Wake up, Peep," they taunted.

"I can't believe she's still out."

"She's tiny," Arach piped up, "You probably gave her too much and her body isn't handling it well."

"And what are you, *traitor*—her protector?"

Silence filled the cells. Peep's mind raced to try to fill the gaps, desperately wanting to know what was happening.

"You could have had it so easy, Arach," one man finally commented. "Your brother could have carried you through life here. All you had to do was play nice."

"And yet, he chose this," the second man tapped the bars casually. "That was a stupid mistake."

"My only mistake was getting caught," Arach replied smugly.

"At least your brother is smarter than you," the first guard laughed.

"He's smarter than all of you," Arach challenged. "And just in case you forgot, boys, some of us were at least skilled enough to not have to be guards."

There was a chuckle in his voice. Peep found herself rooting for the man, even though she still didn't trust him.

The angrier of the guards slammed against the bars, mumbling threats under his breath. The two men argued quietly, making Peep strain to hear.

"Careful, Rowley," Arach warned, "you don't want Piper to think you're colluding with the enemy. You might end up in here with me."

"We're not that dumb," the man responded.

"Sure you're not," Arach chuckled. "At least I was running missions before I ended up in here. What are you doing? *Babysitting*? Have you even been out of the compound since you started working for Piper?"

"Come on, George," the second man said. It sounded like a struggle.

"Come again, boys," Arach called as the man was dragged away.

There was a terribly long pause as Peep held perfectly still.

"You shouldn't taunt him like that," the calmer of the guards returned, speaking to Arach.

"He was going to wake the poor girl up. Don't you think she's been through enough?" Arach asked.

"She's probably about to go through a lot worse," the man answered. "Piper has plans for her. He needs her, but that's the only reason she's still here at all."

"What does he want?" Arach asked.

"You know I can't tell you that." He almost sounded sorry.

"Hey, Mac," Arach got quiet. "Have you heard from him?"

"Your brother? No, but I couldn't even tell you if I had."

Peep held her breath as Mac walked away. His steps grew faint as she tuned in to the sound of Arach breathing. After a long time, he spoke.

"It's clear."

She glanced up just in time to see him bringing his hand back from where he had activated the button tucked away in his collar again.

"Peep," he corrected himself from earlier. "Sorry about that."

"Sure," she rolled her eyes. "Who were your friends?"

"Does it matter?" he asked.

"The one sure seems to hate you," she motioned with her hand to where the men had been standing.

"Rowley? Yeah, he's not my biggest fan. Mac's okay, though."

"What exactly did you do to end up in here?" Peep asked, brushing her hair back.

"Piper caught me. I wasn't exactly holding up my end of the deal."

"What were you supposed to be doing?" Peep examined her nails like she didn't really care.

Arach laughed.

"Not be a double agent, that's what."

Peep's head whipped up.

"Speaking of," Arach smiled sadly, "that brings us to our earlier conversation. We have a mutual friend. *I* know her as Ladybird."

Anne.

Peep turned away, hoping her hair covered the color creeping into her cheeks. Anne had been one of her top operatives until she had disappeared. Peep assumed she had gone dark but hadn't been able to track her down yet.

"I was one of her contacts, Peep. I haven't heard from her in months though." Arach looked away. "Do you know where she is?"

"Ladybird is dark," Peep said, shrugging. She wasn't about to let anyone know that she didn't know where Anne was. The last thing she needed was to get her friend captured. It was bad enough that Fet was out searching for Peep on her own.

"For the record, she was very helpful to me," Arach

rubbed his chin. "Sorry to see she went dark. I hope she has a plan."

Me too.

"Let me see that," Peep nodded toward Arach. He responded with a questioning look. "The button."

Arach subtly took a controlled breath, reaching for the device hidden in the back of his shirt neckline. He pulled the tiny rectangle out and moved toward Peep, passing it through the bars. She took it from him, brushing his hand as she pulled back.

A single button rose up in the center of the small rectangle. Peep rolled her finger over it, noting the tiny indentation on one side. She gently popped it apart, looking at the intricate circuitry inside. It was a masterpiece. She could only imagine the system it connected to.

"My brother made it," Arach admitted.

"I thought he worked for Piper." Peep raised an eyebrow at him as her finger twitched.

"He does," Arach replied, "but he's also protecting me."

Even if *Fet* had done something stupid and betrayed their work, Peep would always try to protect her, so she understood the situation.

"How did you get caught?"

"Piper found my brother, Spider, awhile back. He's a hacker. Actually, he's one of the best hackers. He freelanced for a while but started taking jobs with Piper pretty early on. Eventually, our circumstances changed and Spider had Piper bring me on.

"Now, don't get me wrong, I'm a pretty good hacker myself, but Piper had me running other missions for him. What Piper didn't know was that I was also taking some side meetings and working with people like Ladybird. I kept my head down for a while, but Piper must have suspected something, or someone sold me out, because he had proof I had met with Ladybird. She works for *you*, so obviously it didn't go well for me.

"Spider designed this little contraption and snuck it in after Piper locked me up."

"Your brother's name is *Spider*?" Peep asked incredulously.

"*That's* what you took away from that? Seriously?"

Peep knew there had to have been a reason for Anne going dark. She assumed this was why. As long as Piper hadn't caught her too, Peep wasn't going to press her luck discussing it. If Piper had Anne, she would likely be down here in these cells with her.

"So he caught you," Peep mused, "but your brother is still allowed to work for him?"

"He's the best hacker out there, Peep, and certainly Piper's best. Can you really imagine Piper doing his own work these days?"

"You mean *dirty work*?" Peep rolled her eyes.

"Spider's not bad, Peep." Arach shoulders inched up into a defensive position.

"What exactly were you and Ladybird talking about?"

"Nothing, actually. We had only just met."

"Met how?" Peep tried to be gentle with her interrogation. She failed.

"We really don't have time for this right now," Arach abruptly changed the conversation. "You've got two choices here—ride this out and likely die, or try to get out and *also* likely die. Which angle do you want to play?"

"Hmm, death or *physical exertion and* death? Choices, choices." Peep tapped a finger against her chin as if she were contemplating her decision.

Arach smirked.

"I think I'll take door number three," Peep finally announced.

"Oh? And what is door number three?"

"I'm breaking out."

"You think I didn't try that already?"

"No," Peep cast him a look over her shoulder as she moved toward the bars. "I think you're sticking around here for whatever reason to help your misguided brother."

"You still don't know whose side I'm on," he reminded her thoughtfully.

"I don't really care." Peep shrugged.

The bars were cool against the skin on her wrists as she cautiously reached through, hoping she wouldn't get zapped with an electrical pulse. When she was satisfied, she ran her hand the length of the bars, inspecting everything.

Peep could reach the keyboard on the outside of her holding cell. Her fingers grazed over the plastic buttons. Below it was a second keypad.

"Which one is mine?"

Arach shrugged.

"I honestly don't know. I'm never at an angle where I can tell."

Peep huffed.

"Fine, I'll figure it out," she muttered.

Peep reached into her hair, pulling out what looked like a hairpin. She twirled it in her fingers as she bent down to retrieve the pieces she hid in the bottom of each shoe. She snapped them together, creating a device that would scan the keypad, read the codes, and unlock her door. Had Piper discovered any one of these pieces alone, they wouldn't have amounted to anything. Together, they made her nearly unstoppable.

Arach watched with curiosity as she pieced her techy puzzle together. Peep leaned out of the cell and stretched back toward the keypads. If she were standing outside the cells, hers would be on the left, so logically the top keypad should be hers.

The leader of the Legends placed her toy, a mere

science fair project from a few years back, on the keyboard and waited for it to scan. The device hummed beneath her fingers, clicking to indicate that it was working. Had she not placed it correctly, it would be still until she adjusted it.

The device let out the slightest beep to indicate it was ready. It was so soft that she had to strain to hear it. Peep had designed it to keep the user safe, assuming they were doing something they shouldn't be doing, like breaking in and out of locations.

She pulled the device away, snaking her arm inside to avoid being caught in the moving bars. A loud click sounded, followed by a mechanical swish, but her door remained still.

Peep's eyes darted back and forth.

"No," she breathed. "No, no, no."

Movement to her left caught her eye. Arach's door.

She whipped around to face him, his face white.

He looked at her, head bobbing back and forth between Peep and his open door.

"*What did you do?*" he demanded.

"It should have been mine," Peep muttered.

She threw herself against the bars, arm darting out to the lower keyboard. The device hummed again, clicking silently in her fingers as it worked. The beep sounded, prompting her to pull back.

The whirring noise started again as Peep waited to

make her escape. Instead of her door clicking open, an alarm sounded. Her eyes grew wide as terror washed over her.

"No!" She accidentally shouted out loud.

It had been a trap; the second panel was a decoy. The top controlled them both and her device had found Arach's open code first.

Arach was on his feet, rushing to his door. He darted outside and angled himself back to face Peep.

"Give it," he demanded, thrusting his hand through the bars. "Hurry up."

Confused, Peep handed her device to him. She would lose it one way or the other once Piper's men arrived.

"We have to get you out of here," he slammed the tiny device against the top keypad. "You just blew any chance you had at a quiet escape."

He attacked the bottom keyboard with his free hand, typing in numbers as the device worked its magic. Peep didn't think it would work, but at this point, it didn't matter.

"Come on," he mumbled.

Peep attached herself to the bars, trying to see what Arach was doing.

"Hold this," he finally gave up. Moving a few feet back, he gathered himself before crashing into the bars.

He bounced back, preparing for another run. This

time he kicked out, hitting the bars at the correct angle. The bars bent in, creating a wide gap.

"Once more," Peep directed, hoping she didn't sound like she was begging for her freedom.

Arach directed enough force at the bent bars to create a gap wide enough for Peep to wriggle out . He steadied her as her foot caught.

"We need to run," he said, still holding her wrist.

Arach dragged Peep behind him, rushing down the hall as Peep stumbled with every step. He kept her upright.

"Where are we going?" she gasped.

"I don't know," Arach answered, not even breathing heavily from the run, "Out."

Peep didn't have time to figure out if he was playing her. All she knew was that Arach knew the compound. He knew how to get her out, and right now, he was her best chance.

She hurried to try to keep up, but Arach didn't slow. He darted around corners, took silent hallways, and kept them to the shadows. Peep allowed him to drag her, focusing her attention on finding a screen she could use to hack Piper's system. If she could find a device, she could find a way to protect herself.

Peep slammed into Arach's back as he came to an abrupt stop. It was jarring; as if she were running into an actual wall. He dropped his hold on her wrist, which she assumed would bruise later, and wrapped his arm around her, holding Peep against his back.

He slowly stepped backward, moving Peep back.

"Run," he instructed, turning quickly enough to throw Peep off balance again.

He collided with her, nearly knocking her over as he maneuvered her into the direction he needed her to move in. Once again, they ran, ducking through side halls and up a flight of stairs, this time with men following them.

"You okay?" Arach asked, still not breathing heavily from the run. Peep gasped for air.

"Yeah," she managed to huff between coveted breaths.

"We're about to get caught, Peep. Just do what they say. I'll try to help you." Arach said, slowing slightly.

"Stop," the red-headed guard commanded, weapon raised at them.

Arach stopped them, nearly toppling Peep. She had never seen anyone so agile. No wonder his brother was the better hacker—he must have spent all his time training to be a human shield.

"You really thought you could escape?" the man taunted, walking closer.

"She wanted out." Arach shrugged, still holding her wrist.

Peep panted, nearly doubling over from the run. A metallic taste flooded her mouth as if she had bit down on a metal hanger. It tasted harsh and bitter, but she couldn't summon any spit to her mouth, *let alone* enough to wash the taste away. She cringed as her body shook for more air.

Arach transferred her wrist to his other hand, placing the one between them on her back to steady her as she leaned forward.

"Controlled," he whispered, possibly giving her advice on how to regain the ability to breathe.

"You keep making stupid mistakes," the guard from earlier said.

"You keep saying that, Rowley."

The man standing next to him looking uncomfortable was likely the second guard, Mac. Peep eyed him, taking note of his posture as she looked up, still hunched over, attempting to catch her breath. He seemed familiar but she didn't think they had ever met before. He might be her ticket to freedom later if she could catch him without his partner.

"Let the lady go," the guard with the red hair and giant muscles said. He looked like he could easily match Arach's strength, only he had a weapon.

Arach slowly removed his hands from her, leaving her skin cold. She collected herself and straightened. She would put up a fight.

"Do what they say," Arach reminded her.

The men warily approached them as Arach raised his

hands in surrender. Rowley wrenched Arach's arms behind his back as the other man held his weapon to him. Arach complied, but Rowley still took the opportunity to kick the back of Arach's knees, forcing him to the ground with a grunt.

"Sorry," Mac said, giving Peep a look that begged her not to try to hit him. He added in a whisper, "Just cooperate."

Arach's eyes latched onto her, willing her to go quietly.

Peep relented, allowing the man to bind her hands once again. Her breathing returned to normal as they were escorted back to the main room where she had woken up. She was surprised they hadn't been sent back to the cells, though given the damage they had caused, she probably shouldn't have been.

CHAPTER 3

"I JUST DON'T UNDERSTAND why the two of you insist on making it so difficult on yourselves," Piper mused.

Arach sat in silence, leaning back against the chair. He slouched to accommodate his arms still bound behind his back. Peep perched gracefully on her chair, crossing her legs defiantly. Her fingers stretched down toward her knees as far as they would go. She tapped them against her poofy royal purple petticoat, messing up the rhythm intentionally, making Piper cringe each time he noticed. She reveled in annoying him.

After an hour of sitting with Arach in silence, Piper had finally made an entrance, glaring at them. Peep assumed they were being monitored before his appearance and Arach refused to talk the three times she had tried to whisper to get his attention. Each aggravated sigh earned her a snort that confirmed he was aware of what she wanted and wasn't about to give in.

Peep tapped her fingers from thumb to ring finger, pausing before lifting her ring finger and tapping it again. She repeated the process, ignoring her little finger. Piper sneered, looking away to Arach as Peep laughed to herself. Each time Piper turned to her, she repeated a similar pattern of imperfection.

Arach caught on to her game, tapping his foot every few minutes to irritate Piper. It became a challenge between them to see who could get the best reaction from him as he first lectured, then ignored them.

Peep wondered if Arach had a plan or if he was just messing with Piper. She still needed to find a way out. Piper turned to speak to her, interrupting her thoughts as Mac walked back in. He nodded that Piper should follow.

Piper rolled his eyes.

"What is it?" he shook his head as if he were talking to a five-year old that didn't follow simple directions.

"They're here." Mac finally said, unsure if he should admit that bit of information in front of the captives.

Piper's face lit up with delight, his entire demeanor shifting.

"Well now, that's a different story," he said gleefully.

He tapped the ends of his fingertips together like the old-fashioned villains would do in black and white movies. Peep could picture him dressed in black, wearing a top hat with a curled mustache.

Piper turned to stride out the door. He didn't glance back.

Once the room was clear, Arach moved into action. He rose to his feet, adjusting his hands as low as possible. Sitting on the edge of the seat with his hands below the chair, he worked his way through his arms, contorting his legs to snake his feet through his muscles. With his hands in front of him, he quickly sat back down.

"Play along," he muttered, leaning back against his seat.

Confused, Peep just stared. She had no idea how that had been so quick for Arach. Had she tried to work her arms in front of her, she would have fallen off the chair and caused such a commotion that Piper would have come running back into the room.

Arach sat there as if nothing happened. He stared straight ahead. After a moment, he relented, speaking to her.

"Listen carefully," he said quietly. "They're here, which means they'll be coming for us soon. I don't know what we'll find out there, but they're going to try to use us as leverage. Just keep your head down."

"What do you mean?" Peep gritted her teeth, waiting for an answer she probably wouldn't like.

"You want to get back to your friends, right?"

"Right," Peep confirmed.

"Then keep your head down and don't cause a scene

unless I tell you to. We have to play by their rules for this. Promise me, Peep. Promise you won't pull anything unless I direct you to."

Arach glanced at her from the corner of his eye, attempting to hold his lips still as he spoke. He felt safe enough to communicate, but still assumed they could be monitoring them and took precautions.

"I can't promise that," Peep admitted. "*Who* is here?"

Arach didn't have time to answer. Several guards walked in, weapons ready.

"Up," they commended.

Arach stood quietly, following orders. Peep rolled her eyes dramatically, throwing a little fit before standing. She wasn't going to make this easy on them.

Her dark purple petticoat crashed above her knees when she finally rose, her flouncy lavender skirt moving on top of it. She swished her hands dramatically in front of her, running the backs of her fingers along her skirts to smooth them, making everyone watch her. She smiled sarcastically, tossing her purple and brown locks.

She reached up, angling her elbows to the side so she could smooth down the front of her tailored, button-down shirt. Her brass buttons popped against the light purple dress shirt, the cords making her look like an old-school ringmaster. She could only reach the lowest few buttons with the way her hands were fastened together.

She flashed an award-winning smile laced with

poison at the men. They approached her, grabbing her elbows as the forced her toward the door. She held back her rage and convinced herself not to elbow them. Arach shook his head at her defiance.

"Move," one of the men said.

"LET GO!" PEEP PROTESTED as the men dragged her through the door. She struggled to work against them as they propelled her forward.

It was cool. The breeze smacked her in the face, sending her brown hair whipping back into one of the guard's eyes. He yelped.

"Don't," Arach warned sharply. "Piper needs her."

The man swore behind her.

"What is the meaning of this?" Peep demanded.

Piper stood with a device in his hand. He spoke into a microphone as he watched a picture on his screen. The man strode toward the wall.

When he reached it, a panel slid open revealing the outside world. Grass gently blew in the background, highlighted by the light. Piper's head immediately blocked Peep's view, cutting her off.

"So feisty, Muffet. However do the Legends get anything accomplished with a leader like you?" Piper lifted himself up to get a better view.

Peep gasped. Fet was on the other side of the wall, her muffled voice coming through the now open panel. Piper yelled back, anger and fury overcoming him. Every muscle in his body tensed as he rocked back off his tiptoes.

A male voice answered him back only to have Piper threaten him.

"You'd better pray you can figure out the code then, or your people are dead." He held a hand in the air, ready to signal his guards. Peep prepared herself for whatever that motion might mean for her survival.

"Spider, get out!" Arach yelled, scaring her and the guards.

Two men clamped down on Arach's arms and shoulders, trying to force him to the ground. Even with two of them, Arach held his position.

Whether she could trust Arach or not, she needed him now. Her attention divided between listening for Fet, hoping she would figure out how to pass the plan along to her and trying to silently make a plan with Arach. Barely able to hear Fet, she chose to latch on to Arach's gaze. He was smart enough to know how to break out of captivity and make it through the doors. She hoped part of that plan involved getting the doors open in the first place.

"Who is your leader, Muffet?" Piper yelled. "If you fail, I'll kill them both."

"Not if we kill you first," the man shouted back.

"Tell me who it is!" Piper practically stomped his foot. Peep rolled her eyes at the absurdity.

"Send them out first!"

"I have the code! Send them out!" Fet's voice was chilling. She *couldn't* give the code to Piper.

Over her dead body.

Peep got ready to make a break for it, hoping a solid blow to the man's face as she whipped her head back would give her just long enough to attack Piper. Getting out was no longer her goal, preventing Piper from getting the code was.

"System override in one minute," a mechanical voice filled the yard.

Great, a time limit.

She caught Arach's eye just long enough to start her own count down, mouthing numbers.

The click of the door, followed by a loud whoosh startled them. Everyone looked to the right as their path to freedom magically opened.

There was a change.

Peep could see Fet, kneeling on the ground in her

hot pink plaid skirt, as she leaned over just enough to see inside. Her eyes widened when she connected with Peep.

From that distance, it didn't look like Fet was hurt, but she couldn't be sure.

"Code, Muffet, then you can have your pathetic friends back," Piper leered at her.

"You're so willing to kill for what you want. Is it worth it?" Fet growled angrily at him, looking ready to pounce.

"Fet." Peep glared, willing her to listen.

"Gaining my freedom back?" Piper tipped his head, pretending to be thoughtful. "Yes. It's worth it. After what they did to me...they deserve it. They took everything from me."

"Says the man in a walled-in compound," Fet challenged.

"My price for my silence. No matter though." He tipped his chin slightly to the side, surveying the situation. "It will all be over soon and I can live anywhere I like. I'll control everything."

Peep needed to think of a solution. She should have glanced around to observe anything she could use to her advantage, but her eyes were locked onto Fet. Now that the door was open, it was far easier to hear her.

"You used to protect people," Fet came alive, animatedly speaking. "That's why I'm here, isn't it? Your little failsafe for keeping the system and people protected. What changed?"

"They did," he said, almost sadly. "They took everything from us. So what if there are a few deaths along the way to taking back our system from them? I'm going to set everyone free."

"By ruling over them?" Fet sneered.

"I can keep them safe," Piper said as if he cared.

"By controlling them?" Fet accused the man in front of her.

"By controlling you all." His words were chilling. "Now finish it."

"Fet, don't you dare!" Peep struggled against the guards, knowing it was her only chance. The man next to Fet locked eyes with someone to Peep's left.

"System override in ten seconds."

If Peep could have destroyed the alarm that went off, she would have made that priority even over the codes. She never was one to tolerate alarms.

"Now or never, Muffet," Piper yelled.

The guards raised their weapons toward Peep and Arach, making the situation more dangerous than Peep had anticipated. She knew Piper would never let her out alive, but she had pictured a more dramatic demise for herself.

Fet turned and started entering the code, bending to Piper's will. Enraged, Peep watched. She was horrified that her friend would give control over to Piper just to save her. She wished Piper had killed her earlier and prevented this.

Peep felt dizziness wash over her, as Fet rocked back, no longer pressing the keys. It was done.

"No!" She fell to her knees, dragging the guards down with her.

Seeing an advantage, she broke free, barreling toward the compound. If she could get inside to the system, she might be able to undo the damage, or at least minimize some of it.

"Arach!" a voice yelled moments before she was lifted into the air.

The tall boy spun her, setting her back on her feet as he pulled her toward the door to the outside. She had no choice but to follow as he dragged her along.

A boy with dark hair, long on one side and short on the other, held the door open, wedging himself between it and the wall. Fet raced around him, holding off the guards as Arach pushed her forward.

In a moment of pure insanity, Arach leapt over the boy's legs, propelling Peep forward as part of the jump. She sailed through the air, stumbling as she hit the ground on the other side.

Peep turned just in time to see Fet make the jump. The boy fell as the door closed. Peep's friend pulled the boy along behind her, narrowly avoiding being squished between the closing metal.

"Run," he yelped.

Arach guided them to the tall grass, moving quickly away from the compound. With each step, Peep's anger grew. She held in her screams.

She stumbled twice, catching herself before she fell. It only added to her frustration.

When they finally slowed, she turned on Fet.

"How could you?" she screamed.

"Relax, Peep. You have so little faith." Fet grinned sarcastically.

"She set up a back door," the boy interjected.

Peep's cheeks grew red in fury.

"And just who are you?" She turned to face him.

"That's my brother," Arach turned to her.

"The one that works for Piper?" She attempted to evaluate the situation, still unsure of whom to trust.

"*Worked.*" Spider held up a finger in protest. "Double agent."

"Triple agent." Fet looked amused.

"Wait a minute." Peep realized who he was. "I know you. You're one of the recruits!"

She squinted, looking closely at him.

"Can we skip that and get to the part about the back-door?" Arach redirected, demanding answers.

"Fet used the Irex to create a backdoor," Spider announced.

"Irex?" Arach's shock was obvious.

Peep realized what Fet had done.

"You went…?"

She waited as Fet explained what she had done. Peep was annoyed that Fet had taken Spider to their hidden sanctuary, but she held her tongue.

"Now we have to get back to the Hub and fix this."

"You're sure we can take him down?" Peep asked, praying Fet had set everything up the right way in order to destroy the Piper.

"Now that you're here, I'm positive. You've got the real code, after all." Fet grinned.

"Well then, let's go run the Piper off a cliff." Peep nodded.

CHAPTER 4

PEEP WAS SHOCKED BY the insanity that surrounded the Hub. People were fighting everywhere. *At least it might make a good cover.*

"Stay here," Peep commanded.

They slipped further back into the shadows as Peep made her way toward the building. She crept quietly to the side, sliding along the outside wall until she reached the door.

Breaking in was easy. No one was watching the side door; they were outside, dealing with the masses. The door clicked shut behind her as she glanced around. Taking a breath, she steeled herself and set out to find Nim.

Her contact had to be around there somewhere. He would have transferred to the Hub with the other Coats. Peep just needed to find him without getting caught. Spying a bag on the floor, she made sure the coast was clear and rushed to it. Inside she found what she was looking for.

Entering into a secure channel, she sent a coded message to Nim. Peep dropped the device back inside the bag and settled it back on the floor. She rocked back on her heels to steady herself as she stood.

Nim arrived a moment later, finding Peep attempting to hide in the shadowy corner of the room. He limped inside, brushing his hand through his brown hair.

"I'm here," he whispered once he was sure they were alone.

"I need to get my people inside," Peep said, not bothering with pleasantries.

Nim nodded, taking a step back so Peep could lead.

"Who is with you?" Nim asked as they navigated the halls.

"Fet and two others," Peep responded.

"Who are the others?"

"They're not ours." Peep watched for his reaction.

"Who are they, Peep?" he insisted, momentarily putting a hand on the small of her back to let her know he wasn't giving up on his line of questioning.

"Their names are Arach and Spider," she sighed. "They're brothers."

Nim's head whipped around to face her.

"Wanderers," he whispered.

Peep breathed sharply.

"I know them," Nim said quietly before she could ask. "I've been watching them."

"What do you mean?" Peep asked as they neared the door.

"I had been monitoring them to make sure they wouldn't come after us. There was a raid, but I didn't do anything about it because they weren't Legends. I didn't know how bad it would be until after. Peep," he paused sadly, "most of them didn't survive. That's why they've been so quiet.

"I started watching Spider and Arach after the raid. I wanted to make sure they were okay after losing their family. I've seen them working on the inside. I even helped them out once or twice. They're trying to bring down the Piper."

"That's who did…*this*." Peep waved her hand around, indicating that the madness had been created at Piper's hands.

"I see," Nim nodded, opening the door. He filled her in on more details before adding, "Well, we can trust Spider and his brother. I've watched them long enough to know they would be good assets for us."

"Noted," Peep said as she darted into the open, Nim dropped his limp, keeping up with her.

"He can get us in," Peep announced once she reached Fet and the boys.

When the group arrived at the door, Peep nodded to Fet, letting her know that Spider and Arach would be allowed to continue on with them. Peep lingered behind as Fet and Nim talked quietly. She could tell the moment Fet realized she was talking to Nim, her entire body nearly jumping out of her skin in excitement. She tried to suppress her grin, shaking her head.

When their contact left, Peep positioned herself next to Fet so they could talk. She filled her in on what Nim had told her about their newest members.

"He started watching them and says they are clear. We can trust them." She released her grip on Fet's arm as they found the room containing the Irex.

Peep helped Fet to restore the wires to their proper places, trying to activate the machine that had been disabled as Spider and Arach kept an eye on things.

"What did you use?" Peep questioned.

"The Way," Fet replied.

Peep stepped back with her.

"Seriously? Your plan was to *unplug the cords and use the Way?*" Peep rolled her eyes dramatically.

"Just stop talking and take back the system," Fet waved her hand at Peep condescendingly, making Peep roll her eyes again.

Fet retreated to stand by the boys, allowing Peep space to work. As much as she loved her friend, Peep was not a fan of having people hover over her while she worked. Perhaps that was why she and Fet got along so well—they were similar.

The codes spun, flashing before Peep's eyes in a whirlwind of numbers. Her hands flew over the keys, pounding out codes to counteract the system.

Close.

"Ready," Peep yelped, not expecting to need Fet so soon.

They fought the system together, attempting to regain power from Piper. Altering the codes, they reworked the entire system.

"Spider!" Fet yelled, realizing they needed another set of hands.

Peep had trouble breathing after awhile, warmth building up in the room, multiplied by the odd angle at which the three were bent over the Irex system. Peep bumped into her, accidentally elbowing her. Her fingers nearly slipped, but she caught them in time, avoiding what could have been a disastrous error in the code.

"Almost there," Peep announced when she saw the final parts of the code.

"Don't even think about it," Piper announced, frightening them.

Peep whipped around to find their enemy standing in the room, surrounded by his goons. The guard that had held her right before her escape looked a little worse for the wear, nearly making her grin.

"I knew you couldn't resist doing something like this. So Peep, you're the real leader," Piper taunted her. "I should have guessed. Your stupid act had me fooled. Bravo. But I'm still in control and you're going to step away."

"Not a chance," she tried to say as menacingly as possible.

Something shuffled in the hallway. The cry caught her attention. She knew what was happening even before Piper lashed out his hand and dragged her boyfriend in by his collar. Somehow, Piper had found BB. She was going to slap him for running around looking for her by himself…assuming she could get him out of this.

She gasped as she discovered BB was bound and gagged. He shook his head so ferociously that he nearly lost his glasses.

"Oh, I don't think so," Spider said as he rushed toward Piper.

A fight erupted, everyone taking on guards. Even BB attempted to wrestle away and help. Peep rushed in his direction, hoping to get his hands free so he could fight more easily.

"Take out the machine!" Piper's voice filled the room.

BB pushed Peep back to the console, trying to get her to make the Irex her priority. He forced her to manipulate the codes as he attempted to help, hands still tied. He was pretty fast for being unable to move his wrists apart.

She heard Spider shout a warning to Fet in the background, but didn't have time to look. She pounded on the keyboard until she realized she needed her friend.

"Almost there. Fet!" She summoned Muffet.

Fet bumped BB out of the way, taking over his spot.

"Ready?" Fet asked.

"Now!" Peep set them into action, pressing the final buttons.

Piper became irate as he watched his control slip away, losing his grip on the Barrier program. When Peep turned, she found him shaking in anger.

"*You* did this!" he growled at Fet before running at her to take his revenge.

Peep grabbed onto her friend's arm, attempting to move her out of harm's way, when suddenly, Piper was flying through the air. She smirked as Piper crashed to the floor, not realizing that Spider was close enough to trip him.

The tall, dark-haired boy rushed to Fet's side without so much as flinching from the collision. His face said it all —Peep would be losing her best friend to this man sooner rather than later.

"Go!" He commanded as he protectively gripped her shoulders. "Run!"

Fet started to protest, not wanting to leave.

"Go. Now," Spider insisted. "Arach…"

The eldest brother reached forward, grabbing onto Peep and BB, forcing them to the door. Peep wanted to protest, but Spider's next words silenced her.

"Fet, go," he said urgently. "I will take care of him, but he can't catch you. Now move."

Peep assessed him, wanting desperately to like him

for her friend's sake. She made a mental note to crawl through every digital record of him that there was later if they made it back to the Legends Building. She would know everything about him before she ever let him near Fet.

"No," Fet argued. Peep grinned, knowing Fet didn't like to be babied.

"Get out, now!" Spider yelled as the guards started to wake up. Arach had done a number on most of them. She stepped over a man on the floor as she followed Arach's command to meet them downstairs.

"On it," Arach said, moving toward Fet. She slapped at him.

Peep and BB rushed down the stairs, only hearing a bit of yelling as they fled. Peep ripped at the binds on BB's hands, freeing him before Fet and Arach had reached the stairs.

"Are you okay?" BB's face was white, terrified for his girlfriend.

"I'm fine, what happened?" Peep demanded.

"Later," BB refused to answer. "Did he hurt you?"

"I'm fine," she insisted.

"*Bonita Peep, you tell me the truth,*" BB's words were angry and protective. "Did that man hurt you?"

"You know I hate being called that," she snarled, silently wanting to rip her uncle's throat out for giving her that name.

"Are you hurt?" he repeated, pulling her close to his chest.

He was warm, heart beating rapidly under his shirt. She wrapped her arms around his back, pulling his hips toward her. She didn't realize how cold she was until his arms radiated warmth throughout her back.

"Arach and Spider are fine, we can trust them," she tried to redirect him.

Fet burst through the door at the end of the stairs, looking terrified. Arach followed behind her. Spider was nowhere to be found.

Peep glared, demanding an answer as the watchmen flooded the building to protect the technology and end the intrusion they had only *just* discovered. She hoped Nim would be safe. Spider didn't follow Fet and Arach.

"He stayed behind. We have to go." Arach answered the question she hadn't yet asked.

Newly-freed BB led the way, running all the way back to the Legends Building.

"PEEP!" T SHOUTED as Peep walked in.

She patted the girl's head as T threw her arms around her. After a moment, she detached herself, slipping around the short girl.

She let Fet wander off, knowing she needed a little space. Peep could tell she was worried. Arach hung on the outskirts of the room, watching the scene.

When BB leaned over, Peep grabbed his collar and pulled him close, whispering harshly in his ear.

"I want everything you can find on those two." She released him, giving him a sweet, fake smile for the benefit of the hackers who were watching. "Talk to Nim when he's available."

She motioned Arach over, preparing to introduce him to the group. He hesitated.

"This is Arach," she announced as all eyes turned on him. "He and his brother are the last of the Wanderers. They helped us get the Irex back from Piper and they will be joining us."

The room gasped when they discovered Piper had been in control of the system. T made it her mission to welcome Arach, the rest of the group crowding around him. The boys all watched him skeptically, eyeing his muscular arms. If his hacking skills were as good as theirs, they could be in trouble. Worry was written on their faces.

"He's fine," Peep insisted, knowing they would be leery of him. Spider would fit in better…at least at first.

She realized they already knew Spider.

"Actually, you know his brother. He was one of the recruits. Long and short black hair…"

"Oh," a collective gasp went up.

"He's fine. He was pretending to work for Piper but was actually helping us too."

"Weren't you being held captive?" one of the boys asked. "How do you know?"

"My contact has been watching them," Peep answered. The entire room relaxed, shuffling off to their stations.

"Are we safe here?" Arach asked.

"We're fine," Peep answered, annoyed that he would ask. "We took precautions."

Arach eyed the people watching him from their stations.

"I'm going to go check on Fet," he mumbled.

Peep smirked and gave him directions.

SITTING DOWN AT HER station, she worked her way back into the system to check her work. She wanted to be sure Piper could never get access again. She knew they had destroyed it, but checking one more time wouldn't hurt.

After a while, Arach came back. He reported his brother's arrival, having passed him on his way back. Peep hoped BB's research found nothing and she could be happy for her friend and Spider.

Arach took a seat, looking a little lost. Peep ignored him as she worked, checking over everything they had done.

"Peep!" BB shouted as he ran into the room, holding his device in his hand.

"What?" her head snapped up, fingers stopping in the middle of typing.

"I heard from Nim," he said in a hushed voice. "Something happened."

ACKNOWLEDGMENTS

I know you already love Fet and Spider, but I hope you also enjoyed this look at Peep and Arach! I loved having the opportunity to write their side of the story as well.

While writing Along Came A Spider, I knew a whole world of events were happening behind the scenes for poor Peep as she was held in captivity. What I didn't realize was that I was creating a challenge for myself every time I alluded to her situation in the first book. Making sure everything fit was an interesting part of this follow up. I hope you loved it as much as I did.

I want to hear from you! If you adore Spider, Fet, Peep, and Arach, or if you're a fan of my other writing, reach out to me! The more I hear from you, the more I know what to focus on next. I have multiple projects in the works, but the more I know you, the more I know which ones to spend the most time on...especially since more of The Legends Chronicles is high on my To Do list!

Special thanks to everyone who stuck with me through the craziness that was the release of this book. None of us expected things to happen the way that they did, but I'm so grateful we could all roll with the punches and make this book happen (even if it was months earlier than we had planed!)

Thank you to the wonderful Jody Carr for editing ATCH for me. I appreciate your willingness to jump in and all of your kind words!

To Sissy Lu, you are the best and I truly don't know what I'd do without you! Thank you for all your help!

To you, oh fabulous reader, thank you for jumping into this journey with me. I can't wait to see where it takes us! Until then, I hope you come hang out with me on social media. I have a gift for you over on my newsletter if you if you happen to some free books, as well as other freebie gifts. Come join me at excerpt. kmrobinsonbooks.com I can't wait to hang out with you!

Keep reading for more Legends Chronicles, as well as find out how to get bonus scenes, play an interactive game for the series and more! Plus, I've given you the first chapter of my new series, Virtually Sleeping Beauty, at the end of this book! I have a feeling you're going to like it!

Stay inspired,

-K.M. Robinson

ALONG CAME A SPIDER: THE FIRST PREQUEL NOVELETTE TO THE LEGENDS CHRONICLES

Little Hacker Muffet
sat on her tuffet
destroying her cords and Way.
Along came a hacker named Spider,
who sat down beside her
and frightened his opponent away.

WHEN FET, ONE OF THE MOST SKILLED HACKERS IN THE Legends, discovers her best friend and leader of her group has been abducted and held for ransom, she must escape unnoticed and find Peep before it's too late.

When Spider, a new recruit training to join her hacker ring, slips out with her and claims to have a plan to save her friend, Fet is forced to bring him along. As she discovers he's not who he claims to be, she faces grave danger and learns just how deadly a spider bite can be.

Now available!
Learn more about The Legends Chronicles at
acasinfo.kmrobinsonbooks.com

Think you have what it takes to join Fet and Peep in the Legends? Fet will put you to the test in this choose-your-own-adventure game through Facebook messenger to see if you have the skills to talk your way into the group.

Play now at jointhelegends.kmrobinsonbooks.com and see if you can *hack* it.

BONUS FACEBOOK FILTERS

Want to get your hands on some incredible Facebook filters for Along Came A Spider? Now you have the ability to get filters for the story, characters, etc right inside your phone.

You can use these on your photos, profile pictures, videos, and live broadcasts. All you have to do is like my author page and they will automatically show up in your filters!

I've even taken these clips and put them on Instagram Stories by saving them to my phone and uploading them to Instagram.

Visit www.facebook.com/kmrobinsonbooks to grab these filters for your photos, videos, and broadcasts! Bonus points for tagging me @kmrobinsonbooks so I can see how you're supporting The Legends Chronicles.

ABOUT THE AUTHOR

K.M. Robinson is a storyteller who creates new worlds both in her writing and in her fine arts conceptual photography. She is a marketing, branding and social media strategy educator who is recognized at first sight by her very long hair. She is a creative who focuses on photography, videography, couture dress making, and writing to express the stories she needs to tell. She almost always has a camera within reach.

CONNECT ON SOCIAL MEDIA

facebook.com/kmrobinsonbooks

instagram.com/kmrobinsonbooks

twitter.com/kmrobinsonbooks

Get free excerpts and full novels from K.M. Robinson at excerpt.kmrobinsonbooks.com

ALSO BY K.M. ROBINSON

The Golden Trilogy

Book One: Golden

Forged: A Golden Novella

Book Two: Locked

Book Three: Edge

The Complete Series Boxset/Omnibus with Tempered: an exclusive bonus novella

The Jaded Duology

Book One: Jaded

Book Two: Risen

The Complete Series Boxset/Omnibus with exclusive epilogue

The Siren Wars Saga

Book One: The Siren Wars

Book Two: Darker Depths

Book Three: Beyond The Shores

Origins of the Siren Wars: Prequel Novella

Book Four: Forbidden Waters (coming soon)

The Legends Chronicles

Along Came A Spider: A Prequel Novelette

And They'll Come Home: A Prequel Novelette

The Archives of Jack Frost Series

The Revolution of Jack Frost

The Redemption of Jack Frost (coming soon)

Stealing Steam Series

Book One: Lions and Lamps

Book Two: Pistons and Prisoners

Book Three: Railcars and Rulers

Top Hats and Telegraphs: A Prequel Novella

The Complete Series Boxset/Omnibus with Vambraces and Victories: an exclusive bonus novella

Virtually Sleeping Beauty: A Novella Retelling

The Goose Girl and The Artificial: A Novella Retelling

The Sinking: A Little Mermaid Novella Retelling

Cindrill: A Cinderella Assassin Novella Retelling

Sugarcoated: A Hansel and Gretel's Witch Novella Retelling

Blood Is Silent: A Red Riding Hood Circus Retelling

JADED: BOOK ONE OF THE JADED DUOLOGY

If the only way to stay alive was to convince your new husband not to murder you and make it look like an accident, could you do it?

At eighteen, Jade shouldn't have to be forced to marry the son of her father's enemy as part of a revenge plot for a failed rebellion. When she's thrown into the life of being the wife of the Commander's son and heir, her only hope for survival is convincing Roan Diamond to actually fall in love with her so that he doesn't kill her on his father's wishes.

While a dutiful son, Roan shouldn't have to trick his new wife into believing his family accepts her, but as the only one in a position to make the country believe Jade is part of their family, he will do what he has to before his family murders his young bride and makes it look like an accident to get back at Jade's father.

With half the country trying to protect Jade and the other half oblivious to the atrocities committed at the Commander's hand, it's a race to see who will win at a deadly game of cat and mouse.

One chooses life. One chooses death. In the midst of chaos, only one will succeed.

Now available!
Learn more about The Jaded Duology at
jadedinfo.kmrobinsonbooks.com

GOLDEN: BOOK ONE OF THE GOLDEN TRILOGY

Goldilocks wasn't naive. She was sent on a mission and Dov Baer is her new target.

When Auluria tricks the Baers into letting her into their home, they have no idea she's actually been sent by the enemy to destroy them. Intent on gathering information for her cousin to hand over to the Society seeking to destroy all of the rebel factions—including her own— she's willing to sacrifice Dov Baer to save her people... until she realizes her cousin lied to her.

Now that she's seen who Dov truly is, she has to decide between staying loyal to her only remaining family or protecting the man she's falling for. If her allegiances are discovered, either side could destroy her—assuming the Society doesn't get her first

Available now!
Learn more about The Golden Trilogy at goldeninfo. kmrobinsonbooks.com

**THE SIREN WARS: BOOK ONE OF THE
SIREN WARS SAGA**

War has hovered around the kingdom of Scylla for
generations ever since the original sirens left the mer
collection generations ago after nearly drowning the
human prince. Over the years, select mermaids from the
royal bloodline have been trained as spies to work for the
reigning kings and queens, keeping the collection safe
from sirens and humans.

Celena and her partner, Merrick, work covertly for the
royals—not even her twin brother knows. When they
discover the sirens have broken through the barriers the
mer set up to keep the sirens out, Celena and her friends
must race to the old kingdom of Metten to stop them
from starting a war within their borders.

When she's dragged to the surface, Celena realizes that the war above the waters is as deadly as the one below the waves—and sacrificing herself may be the only way to protect her family.

The Siren Wars have only just begun.

Available now!
Learn more about The Siren Wars Saga at sirenwarsinfo.
kmrobinsonbooks.com

LIONS AND LAMPS: BOOK ONE OF THE
STEALING STEAM SERIES

All wishes require sacrifice...*are you willing to pay the price?*

Cyra spent the last seven years being trained to steal an airship in a brutal competition that leaves the victor with millions. Last year, she won.

Aladdin spent the past year fighting to get enough money to take his mother away from Horallen after his father was murdered. Now, his evil uncle Kacper wants to force him into the competition and straight to his death inside the Collection Cave.

When Aladdin discovers a genie said to have been banished a century ago, the competition becomes even deadlier, and he knows he can't trust the girl who snuck into the competition this year...but Cyra might not survive his ruthlessness either in a game where only the lion's heart can win.

All wishes require sacrifice, and someone is going to pay the price for the Stourbridge.

Available now!
Learn more about The Stealing Steam Series at
lionsandlampsinfo.kmrobinsonbooks.com

ALONG CAME A SPIDER: THE FIRST PREQUEL NOVELETTE TO THE LEGENDS CHRONICLES

Little Hacker Muffet
sat on her tuffet
destroying her cords and Way.
Along came a hacker named Spider,
who sat down beside her
and frightened his opponent away.

WHEN FET, ONE OF THE MOST SKILLED HACKERS IN THE Legends, discovers her best friend and leader of her group has been abducted and held for ransom, she must escape unnoticed and find Peep before it's too late.

When Spider, a new recruit training to join her hacker ring, slips out with her and claims to have a plan to save her friend, Fet is forced to bring him along. As she discovers he's not who he claims to be, she faces grave danger and learns just how deadly a spider bite can be.

22

Now available!
Learn more about The Legends Chronicles at
acasinfo.kmrobinsonbooks.com

THE REVOLUTION OF JACK FROST

NO ONE INSIDE THE SNOW GLOBE KNOWS THAT MOROZOKO Industries is controlling their weather, testing them to form a stronger race that can survive the fall out from the bombs being dropped in the outside world—all they know is that they must survive the harsh Winter that lasts a month and use the few days of Spring, Summer, and Fall to gather enough supplies to survive.

When the seasons start shifting, Genesis and Jack know something is going on. As their team begins to find technology that they don't have access to inside their snow globe of a world, it begins to look more and more like one of their own is working against them.

. . .

Genesis soon discovers Morozoko Industries, but when a foreign enemy tries to destroy their weather program to make sure their destructive life-altering bombs succeed in destroying the outside world, only one person can shut down the machine that is spinning out of control and save the lives of everyone inside the bunker—Jack.

Now available!
Learn more about The Revolution of Jack Frost at
jackfrostinfo.kmrobinsonbooks.com

THE GOOSE GIRL AND THE ARTIFICIAL

WHAT WOULD YOU DO IF YOUR ARTIFICIALLY INTELLIGENT handmaiden stole your identity?

Threatened by her Artificial, Arta, Princess Goselyn is forced to switch places and pretend she isn't human when she reaches Prince Corinth to negotiate a treaty they both need to be able to take their respective crowns one day. If she doesn't comply, her Artificial, controlled by her evil cousin, will not only kill Goselyn's mother, but Prince Corinth and his father as well.

Can the quiet princess outsmart a machine created to be more intelligent than she is, all while surviving the other

Artificials and robots working against her in the foreign palace, or will Corinth and his father find out and destroy her chance to save them all?

26

Learn more about The Goose Girl and The Artificial at goosegirlinfo.kmrobinsonbooks.com

THE SINKING

The sea witch wants to silence her, but not for the reason you think.

WHEN A QUIRKY OLDER WOMAN PAWNS A FANCY SEASHELL necklace at her mother's antique shop on the pier, Cara doesn't think much about the story the woman spins about the wearer turning into a mermaid.

On her way home, she accidentally drops the necklace into the ocean and is swept out to sea where she meets— a merman who volunteers to take her to his mother, the sea queen, to help her get her legs back.

.   .   .

Cara soon learns that it's Quay's eighteen birthday—a day that has been a curse for his family—and is meant to be one for her too. Now she must fight to survive the sea with Quay at her side.

Fans of The Little Mermaid will love this twisted take on the beloved story.

Now available!
Learn more about The Sinking at
thesinkinginfo.kmrobinsonbooks.com

CINDRILL

CINDERELLA IS AN ASSASSIN OUT TO MURDER THE PRINCE...
but he's hunting her too.

The nanobots Cindrill's master gives her to use as a mask allow her to slip into the ball wearing a face that isn't hers, but when the assassination attempt goes sideways, Prince Davin doesn't understand why her face changes when he injures her, slicing her foot open around a unique pair of shoes as she runs away.

When Cindrill runs into the prince the next day without her nanobot mask on, he doesn't recognize her, but immediately decides her skills will be useful on his hunt for the would-be-assassin woman who nearly killed his father and his fiancée the night before.

Both are tasked with the job of murdering the other, but things don't quite go as they had planned when Cindrill's master and Davian's fiancée interfere as the two try to decide whether or not to kill the other.

It's hard to recognize a woman when she uses technology to change her appearance, but Cindrill is going to use that to her full advantage as she destroys the prince. *Will either survive?*

Now available!

Learn more about Cindrill at
cindrillinfo.kmrobinsonbooks.com

SUGARCOATED

Hansel and Gretel's witch was actually on their side...

ANNIKA'S JOB IS TO CREATE A CAKE TO MATCH THE CANDY-colored rooftops, nightly firework shows, and daily parades ending in unexpected executions for the mad king's ball, but her true mission is to sneak a thirteen-year-old assassin into the palace using her gift of illusions.

Hansel's job is to protect his little sister, Gretel, once she assassinates King Levin and ends the destruction in Candestrachen, using his power over light to rescue the young girl from the chaos her influence over life and death will create.

. . .

When the entire forest reconstructs itself under Gretel's command while trying to save herself from a king's guard, Hansel and Annika must put their feelings aside and ensure their plan holds true—even if it means one of them has to sacrifice themselves to protect the mission.

Her illusions were meant to save her....but not everyone will survive the assassination attempt.

Learn more about Sugarcoated at
sugarcoatedinfo.kmrobinsonbooks.com

BLOOD IS SILENT

RED RIDING HOOD IS A CIRCUS AERIALIST AND THE WOLF IS ready to cage her.

Sienna has grown up working for the circus, dangling off her signature red silks every night. Her grandmother has been known to wander off to train new acts for their boss, but when Sienna tries to find her to bring her back to the show, she doesn't expect the dashing and dangerous Elijah to join her.

When they finally find Grandma Ida has been transformed deep in the heart of the woods, Sienna will stop at nothing to save her—but the wolf has her right where he wants her, and she won't be able to escape his claws.

She was told not to go into the woods alone.

Now available!

Learn more about Blood Is Silent at
bloodissilentinfo.kmrobinsonbooks.com

VIRTUALLY SLEEPING BEAUTY

TO WAKE HER UP, HE HAS TO ENTER THE GAME AND HELP HER beat it...

Surely the class president wouldn't illegally over-juice to stay in the virtual reality game citizens are allowed to play for four hours a day, but when Royce's aunt calls in a panic because her goddaughter hasn't left the game yet, his only option is to go inside the game and drag the girl out.

The golden knight quickly discovers the princess' absence in the real world isn't of her own doing—*she's trapped inside the game by unknown forces*—and if she can't escape soon, she could die for real outside of the game. He's even more shocked to discover that Rora outranks him inside of the game, which means she'll have to fight to *protect herself* from the evils locking her inside a dangerous world.

Can Rora and Royce work together to outsmart a vicious queen and evil magician, and defeat digital dragons, or will Rora slowly fade away until there's nothing left but an empty shell and the game ranking she will leave behind?

Now available!

Learn more about Virtually Sleeping Beauty at
vsbinfo.kmrobinsonbooks.com

FIRST LOOK: VIRTUALLY SLEEPING BEAUTY

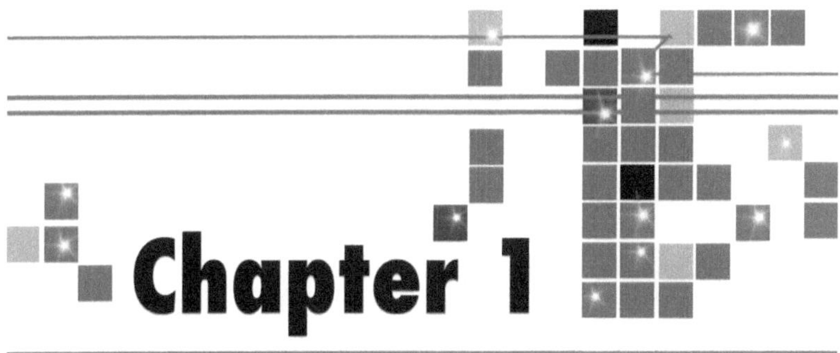

Chapter 1

"I CAN'T GET HER UP," SHE SOUNDS PANICKED.

"You can't *what*?" I mumble.

"I can't get her up, Royce. You need to come over here and help me."

She sounds like she's rushing around the room.

Suddenly, I hear the sound of skin coming in contact with skin as she taps her goddaughter's cheek repeatedly as she tries to wake her.

"Would you relax please, Aunt Perry? She's in a game. She'll be under for a while. That's just how virtual reality works these days—once you're in the chair, you're out for up to four hours depending on your settings."

I jingle my keys to my car, trying to flip to the correct one. It's ridiculous how many different keys I have to carry for my family.

"That's the problem, Royce. She's been in there since this morning."

I glance at my watch. 3 pm.

"What *time* this morning?" A twinge of nervousness slips into my voice. I don't exactly know this girl, but that fact that she's been in for over four hours has me concerned.

"Eight. She was supposed to be out for lunch. We had errands to run."

Perry murmurs something to the girl, this time slapping her harder.

"Perry, stop!" I shout. "That's not going to help."

"What about water—?"

"No!" I bellow. "Just stop messing with her. I'll be right over."

I drop my coffee cup into the drink holder before

slamming the keys into the ignition. The car roars to life —*the red-hot beauty that she is*—and I take off down the block.

Aunt Perry's house is only a few streets away but by the time I arrive, she's in the driveway waving hysterically at me. I take a deep breath to steel myself.

"Royce, I don't know what's happening," she sobs as she grabs my arm, pulling me toward the house. My coffee sloshes out of the mouthpiece of my container, dripping on my hand. Good thing it wasn't that hot to begin with.

We stumble up the steps clumsily as she pulls me into the house. My father's siblings have never been known for being great in a crisis. She pulls me toward the stairs inside and I managed to pull free of her so I can walk with my drippy hand on the banister.

"Calm down, we'll handle it," I demand a little more aggressively than I mean to. Perry looks close to tears. "I'm sorry. We'll figure this out, I just need you to stop shouting."

She nods, holding back the tears.

"Okay, tell me what happened," I prompt.

"Rora has been staying with me this week while her parents are on their trip," Perry starts, gaining the tiniest semblance of the ability to speak. "Once or twice in the evenings she's played her game for an hour, but she always comes down to have ice cream with me before we go to bed."

None of this is helpful, but okay.

"Because it's the weekend, she usually gets up early to play, so we had planned on her playing until eleven and then we were going to go get lunch and run some errands. When I came to check on her a little after eleven, she was still in the game. I assumed she started late so I gave her an extra hour."

She tugs me over to the sleeping girl in the chair, sniffling.

"It's been hours, Royce. I can't wake her up. What do we do?"

"Some people have been known to take extra injections to stay in longer," I offer.

"She wouldn't. She's too responsible for that." Perry gives me an impatient look. "This is the girl who is class president, and works at charities, and does all of her homework for the entire week before she even *considers* playing a virtual game. Rora wouldn't take extra injections when she knows it's against the rules."

Some people are adrenaline junkies—they do it for the rush. Maybe Rora is one of those girls who is super straight-laced in all other parts of her life and this is her guilty pleasure.

I can't say that would be the *worst* thing in the world. I, myself, would love to stay in the games longer.

"Well, if that's the case, maybe we should call a medical team to come wake her up," I reply, turning for the door. Let them handle her.

"No!" Perry shouts, racing after me. "We can't. If something really *did* happen, we can't let them catch her. And even if she hasn't done anything wrong, her mother's going to kill me for letting this happen on my watch. Please, Royce, we need a better idea."

I sigh dramatically.

I don't like being at everyone's beck and call.

"Fine, there's one other thing we can do first."

Setting my coffee cup on the desk next to a few of the girl's binders, I walk back over to where she's quietly laying in the chair.

She's still breathing, which is a good sign. Her fingers twitch slightly so I can tell she's playing the game. Other than that, she barely moves—a side effect of the injections that allow us to enter the virtual world and feel and experience everything inside the game.

"I'll go in and find her," I announce.

"What? No, Royce, you can't." My aunt pulls on my arm. "What if you get stuck in there too?"

"I won't. I do this all the time." I brush her off. "Go grab me an injection, would you?"

After an angry look, she turns and leaves to find an injection.

Most people use the virtual reality system in one form

or another, so there are usually injections lying around every house. The older generation uses it to relax—sometimes they go to a beach, other times they attend orchestra concerts or explore museums. The younger generations are more careless and play high intensity games. I tend to spend my time gaining skills I'll never use in real life as I leap from buildings and save damsels in distress.

I climb into the chair next to her and roll up my sleeve. When I have my feet comfortably arranged at the end of the footrest, I lean back and make sure I like the position I'm sitting in.

Perry walks back in and hands me the injection.

"I'm going to set the machine for an hour, but hopefully I'll find her right away. I need to get over to Alan's, so I don't have a lot of time to waste."

Perry looks nervous so I send her downstairs with the assignment of running her errands for the day. I promise to call her when I have her houseguest back in the real world. She reluctantly agrees to leave, slowly walking out the door to her car. An empty house is for the best right now.

I wait for her to drive away. The last thing I need is for her to come back in, have a meltdown, and throw water on me while I'm in the game. I quietly study the girl's face while I wait so that I don't accidentally miss her in the game. It's a little hard to see around her goggles, but it will suffice. I program the machine to take me to the game she is playing.

With the headset on, ready to be slipped over my eyes, I place my hand on the reader to identify myself and then inject my arm. I quickly put the goggles in place and rest my hands on the arms of the chair.

My vision goes black before crackling into a white burst of light. It fizzles out as the gamescape filters into place in front of me.

Interestingly enough, Rora plays the same game that I do. That should make this easier.

I glance down at my armor to make sure everything is in place. My weapons are just as I left them, attached to the quiver on my back. When I'm sure nothing glitched on me, I walk forward into the game, leaving the holding cell behind. It disappears behind me, evaporating into the air, leaving me exposed.

I quickly flip my settings to explore mode, preventing me from losing any of my credits in the game. I can't engage with people and earn items within the game, but I can walk around and talk to them. It's not something the game allows you to do for extended periods of time, but occasionally people use the setting to meet with their friends while they were in different locations, so the game gives us some leniency while we wait for people to show up.

Now, I just have to figure out where to find the girl.

Virtually Sleeping Beauty is now available at vsbinfo.
kmrobinsonbooks.com